There's a HOUSE inside my MUMMY

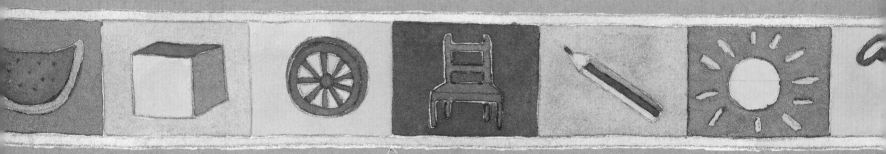

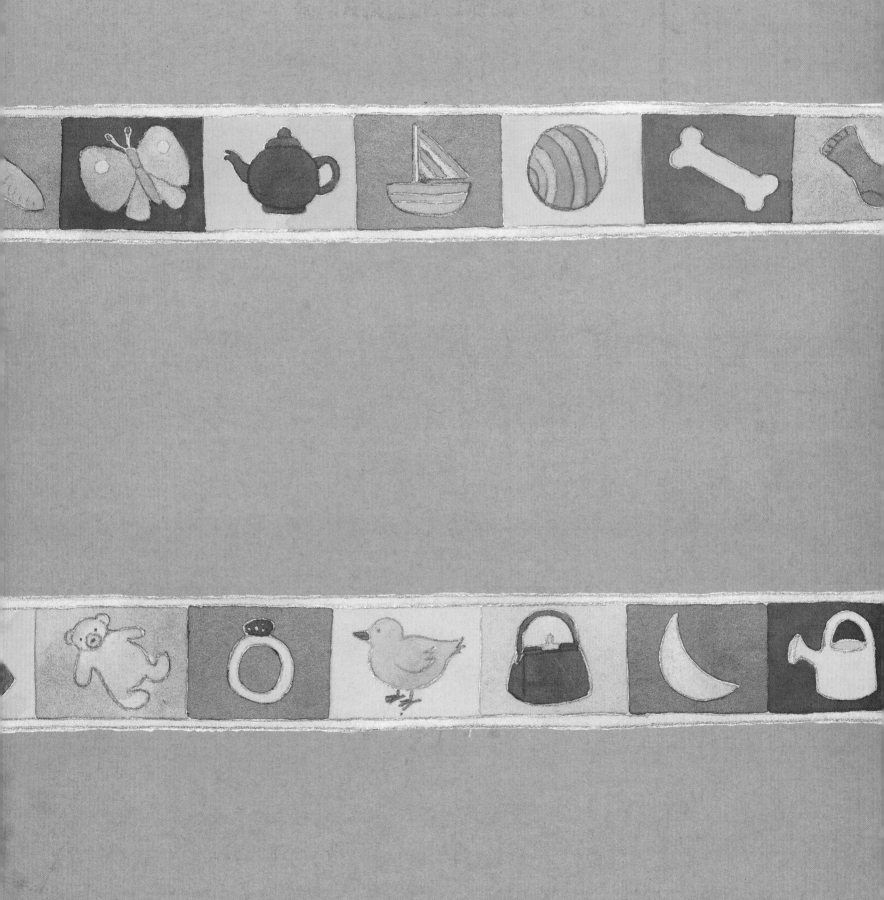

For Victoria, Flinn, Freya and Nat
G.A.

For Melanie, Gerry, Jack and Luke
V.C.

ORCHARD BOOKS

Carmelite House, 50 Victoria Embankment, London EC4Y 0DZ

First published in 2001 by Orchard Books

First published in paperback in 2002

Text © Purple Enterprises Ltd, a Coolabi company 2001 coolabi

Illustrations © Vanessa Cabban 2001

The rights of Giles Andreae to be identified as the author and
of Vanessa Cabban to be identified as the illustrator of this work have been
asserted by them in accordance with the Copyright, Designs and Patents Act,
1988. A CIP catalogue record for this book is available
from the British Library.

ISBN 978 1 84121 068 1

32 31 30

Printed in China

MIX
Paper from
responsible sources
FSC
www.fsc.org
FSC® C104740

Orchard Books, an imprint of Hachette Children's Group

Part of The Watts Publishing Group Limited

An Hachette UK Company

www.hachette.co.uk

There's a HOUSE inside my MUMMy

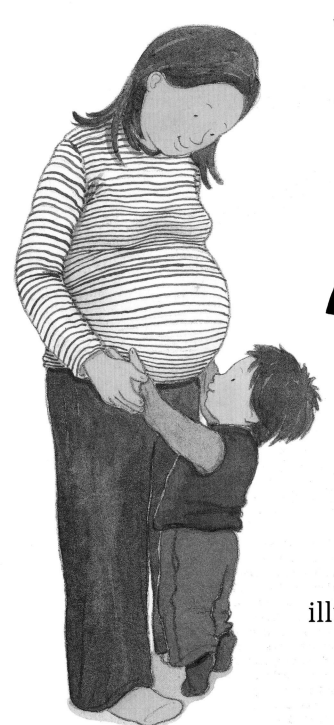

written by
Giles Andreae

illustrated by
Vanessa Cabban

ORCHARD

There's a house inside my Mummy
Where my little brother grows,
Or maybe it's my little sister
No one really knows.

My Daddy says I lived there too
When I was being made,
But I don't remember very much
About it I'm afraid.

He always likes to tell me
It's a lovely place to be,
He knows because he's seen it
On the hospital's T.V.

It's very warm and cosy
But because there's not a bed,
There's a sort of giant bathtub
Where the baby sleeps instead.

He needs to have a lot of room
To help him grow and play,
And that's why Mummy's tummy house
Gets bigger every day.

It's got to have a kitchen
So he doesn't get too thin,
And I think the food my Mummy eats
Can find its way to him.

He seems to want such funny things
But Mummy's very kind,
So she eats all sorts of crazy stuff
And doesn't seem to mind.

I try to help look after her
And see she gets some rest,
Often she falls fast asleep
Before she's got undressed.

Sometimes Mummy feels so sick
I don't know what to do,
But if I had a house in me
I'd feel quite poorly too.

I wish the house had windows
So that we could see inside,
I couldn't find a single one
However hard I tried.

I'd like to show him all my toys
And let him see the view,
And point out all the brilliant things
I'll teach him how to do.

Sometimes me and Mummy
Like to cuddle on our own,
And I tell him that I love him
Through her tummy telephone.

I'm sure that he can hear me
And he likes the way I sound,
'Cause we see him kick his little feet
And somersault around.

I just can't wait to meet him
I hope that he's all right,
My Daddy says be patient
As his door is rather tight.

Look who Mummy made for us -
My lovely little brother!
There's no-one in her tummy now...
UNTIL SHE MAKES ANOTHER!

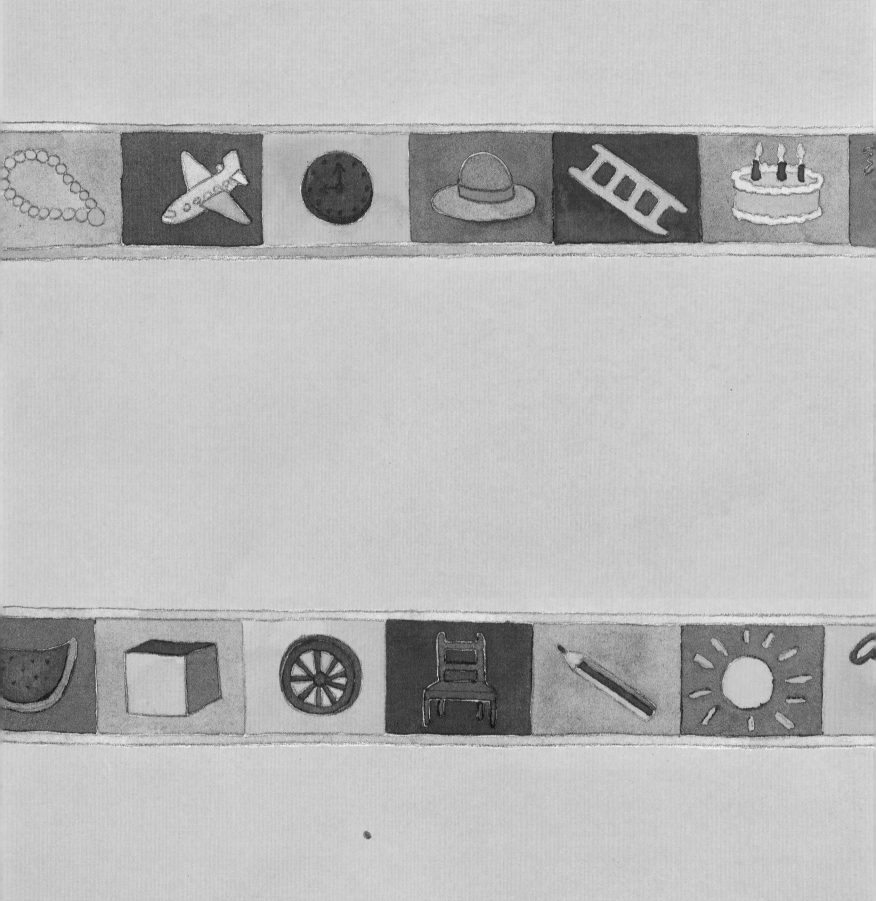